Copyright ©2022
Missing Piece
by the author writing as Elle M Thomas

All rights reserved.
The moral rights of the author have been asserted.
No part of this publication may be reproduced, distributed, or transmitted in any form or by any means, including photocopying, recording or other electronic or mechanical methods without the prior permission of the author, except for brief quotations embodied in critical reviews.

This is a work of fiction.
Names, events, incidents, places, businesses, and characters are of the author's imagination or used in a fictitious manner.
Any resemblance to actual persons, living or dead, or actual events is purely coincidental.

Cover design: Wingfield Design
Formatted: VR Formatting

Chapter One

Gideon

"Tell me this is a joke?" Even as I asked the question, pleading for it not to be true, I knew this was deadly serious. My old man had known exactly what he was doing when he'd added this clause to his will.

"Afraid not, Mr. Knight. Your father was most insistent."

"I bet he was, the old bastard."

"Maybe we should contest the will. I mean these are not the actions of someone of sound mind, are they?" my solicitor and friend, Simon asked, and he had a point, a really good point, but my father had been many things but none of them were mad.

My father's solicitor of the last thirty years, John Barrington, looked ready to object to Simon's words, but he didn't need to, I did.

"No, he knew what he was doing."

The sound of the door knocking was followed by people entering, legal people and then her. Madison Forbes. Fuck me, she was beautiful, of that there was no denial, but when I looked at her face, the scowl fixed there, I remembered why we had never got on.

THE NEXT HOUR PASSED, ALL OF US TAKING IN THE DETAILS of my father's last will and testament.

"So, to clarify." Madison sat up a little straighter in her seat. "In order to regain *my* father's original company, I have to work with him." Her head twitched towards me.

"Correct, Miss Forbes," Barrington confirmed.

Madison scowled at me as if this was my idea of fun. It wasn't.

"I'm not what you'd called thrilled either," I told her, causing her brows to knit together and her face to contort into something resembling distaste.

She huffed and for some reason that made me smile.

"You think this is funny?" She was steaming now.

"No, but knowing how much this pisses you off is satisfying."

Her mouth opened but it was Barrington who spoke again. "There is a final clause and this, as with the working relationship, is non-negotiable."

He had our rapt attention once more but neither of us could possibly have been prepared for his next words.

"The two of you must live together in the former family home for no less than a year."

"Fuck you, fuck him, and fuck you, too." Madison was on her feet and preparing to leave, her final *fuck you* aimed at me.

I couldn't help but admire her balls even if it did distract me slightly from the final detail of my father's last wishes. Her balls distracted me less than the gentle swing of her hips that were encased in a simple grey shift dress.

"Miss Forbes, in the event that you decline alone, all of the estate goes to Mr. Knight, including the assets you currently have from all of Knight Inc. and its subsidiaries.

She stopped dead and spun to face the room again. "But my home, my business, my life . . ."

"Those are the terms." Barrington looked guilty, and why wouldn't he? He had drawn this will up and knew it was blackmail, pure and simple.

"Surely–" I began, unsure what I was going to say, but I didn't want her life as she had so melodramatically put it.

Barrington cut me off. "No. No exceptions and the same clause is in place for you. You refuse and you lose your assets from Knight Inc. and any subsidiaries."

"Now, hang on. I run the business, have done for years. Fuck it! I am the business." My protest was met with a shake of the head from Barrington and a snigger from Madison. "You think this is funny?" I repeated her words.

"No, but knowing how much this pisses you off is satisfying." She looked smug as she threw my earlier words back at me.

"So, this deal is for a year and then we can go our separate ways with our own family business?" I couldn't believe I was considering this, but what choice did I have?

"Yes," Barrington replied and then dropped the biggest bombshell of all. "And of course, you can then divorce."

"Divorce?" Madison and I screeched the one word in stereo.

"Oh, sorry, did I not make that clear. You will marry before the end of the month and the year will run from the day of the wedding. You will live to the outside world as a

3

happily married couple, but after the year is up, you decide how you proceed."

I had no words and neither did Madison judging by the heavy silence that hung between us.

"I'll leave you both alone to discuss things."

The room quickly emptied leaving us alone, looking at each other. Neither of us spoke for long, awkward minutes and then it was her that did.

"Sorry about your dad. My mother loved him and despite the way they got together, I never wished him dead."

I nodded, unsure what to say in response. "Thanks." The way they'd got together involved her mother, a widow, becoming my father's mistress and eventually his wife, ending my own parents' marriage. She had brought into the marriage her late husband's business and when she died, five or six years ago, the business had gone to my father, not his daughter who sat opposite me. The same business that should have gone back to Madison now, without conditions, something everyone assumed would be detailed in the will reading . . . clearly that wasn't in my father's plans. I had taken over our own family business after Madison's mum, Helen, had died and the old man had lost interest in things generally, and here we were.

"This can't be legally binding," she said, suddenly springing to her feet and pacing the length of the table we sat at. "If we contest it legally, or even go to the press, surely someone will see the madness of it, the inappropriateness. For God's sake, say something," she cried at me.

"I won't have people viewing him as a mad old man. He was as sane as you or me, well as me." I couldn't resist a dig.

She ignored it. "Then the press–"

I cut her off. "And have him publicly ridiculed? No."

"Then what?"

"I don't know."

She pulled her phone out. "Then I am talking to the press."

I was before her and snatching the phone from her grip in the blink of an eye. "No. No fucking press. If we fight this and he comes out of it unscathed, we may not win and then the cat's and dog's home will never want for anything again."

I watched her face change as realisation dawned.

"So, you with all the answers, what do we do?"

"Looks like we're getting married."

She closed her eyes as if in actual physical pain. I knew we had never hit it off . . . okay, I had been openly hostile from the second I met her, but the thought of being married to me, living and working with me for a year wasn't that abhorrent, was it?

"Be serious, Gideon."

"I am being serious." I was. From where I stood, there was no other option.

"No! You're being ridiculous, almost as ridiculous as your idiot father and this ridiculous plan for blackmail."

"Then walk away, Madison. I'll take care of your business." She was pissing me off with her attack on my father, even if I couldn't entirely disagree with her accusations. "And his idiocy and ridiculous plans didn't stop your mother dropping to her knees before him, possibly literally."

"Fuck you!" she screamed, stepping closer.

And although I knew her *fuck you* wasn't an offer, I

couldn't resist antagonising her and this situation a little more. "The apple doesn't fall far from the tree, does it? But the old man didn't stipulate fucking. Not that I won't throw you a bone if desperation strikes, darling."

The sound of her hand colliding with my face echoed around us and I swear, my head spun. Turning, she was standing at the exit, throwing the door open and calling to the legal people waiting for us. "Get yourselves a hat. We're getting married." She turned back and glared at me rubbing the burning skin on my face. "Three-hundred-and-sixty-five days, and I intend to make each and every one a living hell for you, darling."

Madison

"You don't have to do this. We will find another way . . . there has to be another way." My friend, and my witness for the day, Josie, stared at me as I added the final touches to my make-up.

I looked at her and smiled. I did have to do this. I had no choice, thanks to Lucas Knight, my deceased stepfather. He had manipulated people in business his whole life, and now he was having one last go, but this time with me and his son. My mother had adored him, and it had been entirely mutual. I could only dream of having someone look at me the way he'd looked at her. Shaking ideas like that from my mind, I refocused on my mascara. The irony that today, my wedding day, should have been the day I was looked at that way didn't escape me.

"Josie, I'm getting married."

She shook her head. "A year is a long time to be unhappy."

"And a lifetime is a long time to be poor." I sounded harsh, brash, and totally materialistic. Although I didn't want to lose my lifestyle, this wasn't about money. "A lifetime is also a long time to know that the business my father built from nothing is being run by Knight Inc. Please, can you just be here for me and even if you don't understand, support me?"

"Of course." She reached for me and holding my hands in hers, looked down at my white dress and smiled. "You look beautiful."

"Thanks, but it will be wasted on Gideon."

She shook her head. "I doubt that. He might be your enemy, but he is a man, and a man of good taste, so, he will notice."

I laughed and shook my head. Gideon was gorgeous in every way physically, tall, broad, dark, brooding and beyond handsome, but his personality made him ugly to me, or at least the personality he showed me. The wider world, the beautiful women, models, actresses, socialites, heiresses, they got the physically gorgeous as well as the matching personality. The injustice of that still stuck in my throat. He despised me based on my mother's actions, her affair with his father that had led to his parents' marriage ending. The unfairness of that was that somehow I was held accountable for our parents actions in a way his own father wasn't.

I needed not to think of this today or I might just bail. "That's of no consequence, and I'm unsure if I want him to notice."

"What if the sight of you gives him blue balls?"

I laughed even louder now. "Okay. Maybe him noticing may not be all bad because for the next year he isn't getting any from anywhere or anyone, so, perhaps his balls will drop off."

Josie looked shocked at that clause of the will.

"Didn't I mention that? We have to be faithful for the year, too."

"Shit, never mind his balls, what about your needs."

I shrugged. "That's what vibrators are for. Now, let's go and get married."

WHEN I WALKED INTO THE SMALL ROOM OF THE HOTEL where we were to marry, I noticed Gideon immediately. I mean, it would have been difficult not to as there were no more than eight people there including me. Gideon had Simon as his witness and best man and along with Josie and me there was Lucas' solicitor John Barrington and another man and finally two registrars.

Gideon looked his usual gorgeous and perfectly put together self. He wore a dark blue suit with a sparkling white shirt and a dark tie. His hair was styled into messy waxed perfection and as I approached, I swore I could smell him. That was something nobody could deny about Gideon Knight, he smelt like heaven on earth. His blue eyes seared through me when I came alongside him, and unable to decipher the meaning behind them and his hard swallow, I dropped my gaze and focused on his shoes. Italian leather that shone like the sun. Even his shoes were perfect. I swore if you looked up tall, dark, and handsome, you would find a photo of Gideon . . . or maybe tall, dark, handsome and a bit of a dickhead, but still.

The service began with the registrar welcoming everyone. I had to study his face to decide if he was being sarcastic. He wasn't. Like Gideon and I hoped the rest of the world would be, he was convinced this was real. The reality hit me at that second and butterflies nervously began to flutter in my stomach and chest. As if sensing this, or possibly feeling the same way, Gideon glanced across at me and with the tiniest of half-smiles, he took my hand in his. Maybe he wasn't a complete dickhead after all. That thought was replaced with concerns about whether my nervousness had made my hand that he was holding clammy.

I returned his smile and wanting to avoid the intensity of his gaze, returned my attention to the registrar.

The wedding ceremony was brief and to the point. We were married and although the sentiments of forever, love and devotion were uttered by us both, we knew that wasn't what we were committing to. There were no positive feelings or a timeline beyond the next year. It was a business transaction, no more. The exchange of rings had surprised me. I hadn't expected Gideon to have one, but he had, and now we both wore matching plain platinum bands, mine a narrower version of his.

JOSIE AND I WERE STOOD TOGETHER, EACH OF US NURSING a glass of champagne, although mine tasted slightly bitter. Gideon and Simon stood nearby in the luxurious but intimate hotel function room next to the room where our wedding had taken place when there was a knock at the door, startling me.

Gideon strode to the door and returned a few seconds later with a man and a woman, the man carried several cameras, and the woman . . . shit! I recognised her. She was a celebrity journalist, blogger, vlogger, and every other title I could think of along with gossip monger. Turning my back on her, I glared at Gideon who had the audacity to smile at me. Not a normal smile, but his most charming, adoring, panty melting smile. Arsehole.

"Darling," he called, sidling up to me where he slid an arm around my middle, pulling me in tight. "I know you wanted to keep things lowkey and personal, but I couldn't wait to shout the news from the rooftops, so I asked Maria to join us for a little exclusive."

What could I say to that without blowing this ridiculous fake relationship out of the water? Nothing, that's what. He didn't need to say anything else, but of course, this being Gideon, he did.

He released me and dropped slightly, tilting my chin up so we were eye to eye. "Don't be mad at me, darling."

I hated that fucking *darling* we had both used on the day of the will reading as an anti-term of endearment. To anyone witnessing it, it appeared to be a loving name, but we both knew differently.

His gaze was still on me. "Tell me you forgive me for wanting the world to know you're finally mine?" Then, he leaned in to land the tenderest of kisses to my lips that were fortunately closed, or else I couldn't have guaranteed that I wouldn't have responded in kind.

I smiled, although it felt more like a grimace. This was

day one and he was already driving me insane. How the fuck was I going to last a year with him?

Chapter Two

Gideon

Madison was absolutely seething. I could see and feel it as we sat together, talking to Maria Ferguson, renowned gossip columnist and scandal stalker. This seemed like a good idea when I hatched it with Simon. The terms of the will stipulated that we had to marry and to the outside world portray the image of perfect newlyweds, so, who better than Maria to confirm and circulate that myth. I'd decided not to run it past Madison first. One, because I had a feeling she wouldn't agree to it, and two, because I wasn't in the habit of running my decisions past anyone.

She laughed, distracting me. I turned and watched as she began to discuss the idea of having tamed me with Maria, who was eating out of her hand. Madison was gorgeous by anyone's standards but as she sat next to me, her hand tucked in mine as part of this charade, her hair a mass of soft, golden-brown curls piled on her head, her make-up barely there showing off her natural beauty, she was breath-taking. I allowed my eyes to dance down the length of her body that was perfectly proportioned with curves and softness encased in white lace. I even allowed my glance to drop as far as her feet that were wrapped in white strappy, heeled sandals that fastened at her ankles that were visible. Even her ankles were attractive.

"Gideon!" Madison's voice carried warmth and humour, startling me until I realised Maria's eyes were fixed on me, meaning the gentle and playful nature of this exchange was all for her benefit, none of it real or for me.

I was seriously losing the plot. This was day one of the next year and she was already fucking with my head because I neither needed nor wanted Madison Forbes' positive attention. This was not real. This was fake and we both knew it. Our motivation was the same, money and business. Fuck me! She wasn't Madison Forbes any longer. She was Madison Knight.

Maria laughed along with her as I returned my full attention to them both.

"I was just saying that there is a lot to love about your wife, but your eyes appear to be ahead of me with your admiring glances and secretive smiles." Maria quirked an eyebrow, pleased to have caught me out in my admiration of my . . . wife. Shit! I had an actual wife!

"Indeed," I managed to utter before regaining my composure ready to answer more questions about how the established relationship between Madison and me had turned romantic.

I waxed lyrical for the next thirty minutes about our love story, the details of which were a figment of my fertile imagination and judging by the doe-eyed expression and gasps of delight she uttered, Maria was buying it entirely. For a split second, as Madison gave me a coy sideways glance, I could have sworn she believed it too.

We posed for countless photos and discussed our romance again and again. I even managed to suggest that our surprise wedding with a lack of guests had been done due to the recent death of my father and Madison's lack of either parent. When Maria had asked about my mother, it had taken me a few seconds to recover because I knew I would never have been able to lie to her about this, so, I hadn't told her. It wasn't unknown for me to act spontaneously, and I hoped that would be how my mother saw it when she discovered I was married. I knew my choice of bride would give her a jolt, but because of my hostility to Madison rather than my mother holding her in any way responsible for the break-up of her marriage to my father. That was a conversation I'd had with Mum on many occasions, that Madison had been innocent in her mother's affair with my father. As innocent as me, and yet, just seeing her made me irrationally irked and antsy. I ignored the voice in my head telling me that the whole of the next year was going to see me being beyond irked and antsy. Maybe I could learn to forget who she was, or at least who her mother was.

"I think we're all done here." Maria was offering a hand as she smiled at us both.

In turn we accepted and then, she passed a final comment, one that startled Madison judging by how she stiffened next to me.

"Have a wonderful honeymoon. I'm assuming I won't get the exclusive on that." She laughed, as did I, unlike Madison who stared at the other woman. Fortunately, Maria saw it as something akin to shock or embarrassment at what a honeymoon was. "Oh my, your face, bless you.

Well, thanks for this and maybe I'll be back in around nine months." She winked and then she left.

Madison

I WAS MARRIED TO GIDEON KNIGHT AND THE WHOLE world was about to discover it courtesy of Maria Ferguson. The afternoon had been surreal in epic proportions. Gideon had given the performance of his life when discussing our brief but intense courtship that had led to him proposing and insisting on a speedy wedding. I'd almost believed it myself. Maria had made several comments about him having been the country's most eligible bachelor and how our marriage would break a million hearts. The pang in my chest as I imagined all of the women he'd been with had shocked me, and now, several hours later, I was still a little startled by it, but then, today had been a strange day.

"Penny for them."

I looked across at Gideon who appeared to be studying me in the back of the car we were travelling in.

"Nothing." I shook my head as if shaking the thought from my mind. "Where are we going?"

"Surprise." He grinned and then it was gone as if he had suddenly remembered who he was speaking to.

We remained silent for the next half an hour or so and then we came to a dead stop. The door opened and the driver waited for Gideon to get out. He then held his hand out. Instinctively, I took it and found myself standing in front of a plane, a private plane with the discreet but distinctive logo of Knight Inc. subtly placed. With my hand still in his, Gideon led me towards the stairs. Like a lamb to the slaughter, I followed. The driver muttered something about having a nice time, but that was as much as I heard before finding myself at the entrance to the plane where a couple of flight attendants and pilots stood.

"Mr. Knight," the first pilot said, extending a hand to Gideon and then me. "Mrs. Knight."

Oh my God! I was Mrs. Knight. That was how the world was going to view me, as his wife. I mean, I knew I was. That's what I had agreed to but knowing that's how everyone else would see me had hit me like a ton of bricks. No! I wasn't having it. I was Madison Forbes, and that was how I intended to stay.

I took the hand offered and corrected him. "Ms. Forbes."

Gideon's grip on my hand tightened, uncomfortably so. "Mrs. Knight and I will be on board." He pulled me along and said nothing until we were in our seats, me with an untouched glass of champagne and him with a scotch on the rocks.

"You are Mrs. Knight. Whether you like it or not, you are, the world will view you that way, and I won't have you making me look stupid by denying it."

I stared at him sitting opposite me, wondering why this mattered to him. "This is not real, Gideon, and in exactly a year, it will be over, and I will be Madison Forbes to the world once more, but to me, I have never been and never will be anyone else."

He held my gaze, his eyes flickering with something I'd never remembered seeing before, confusion, empathy, guilt? And then as his mouth opened, it was gone. "Yeah, but for the next year, you are my wife, Mrs. Knight, so get used to it."

"You are a fucking arsehole and I hate you," I spat, turning away from him as a flight attendant appeared to tell us we were about to take off to fuck knows where. "It's going to be a very long year."

"No fucking kidding!" he said, my focus back on him as he reached for his glass and downed his whiskey. "Now buckle up for the ride."

I had no clue whether he was referring to the next year or the flight, but whichever it was, I did indeed need to buckle up.

Chapter Three

Gideon

We hadn't spoken much since our exchange on the flight, but as we arrived at our private villa in the South of France, I decided that we were in this together and for the next year we were stuck with one another, so maybe we needed to clear the air. The problem with clearing the air was that it could go wrong and then we'd be stuck in the middle of more tension and bad feeling. I didn't want that and knew she didn't either, so maybe rather than clearing the air, I'd extend a white flag.

Climbing the stairs of the villa, we made our way to the master suite. Seeing the huge bed dressed in white linen and the sea view via the open doors to the terrace, Madison froze.

"You want . . . you expect . . . we . . . together."

I smiled at her, but not in a smug one-upmanship way, happy to see her discomfort and struggling for words. No. I smiled because this was my opportunity to wave the flag I'd earlier decided we needed.

"No, of course not. I know we have to be the perfect newlyweds to the outside world, and we will, but behind closed doors, when it's just the two of us . . ." my voice trailed off and I risked a glance down at her. How glad was I when I saw her warm and genuine smile? I pushed the idea of her smile being down to relief at not having to share a bed with me, and simply focused on her beautiful face, her hair scraped up in a high ponytail, her bright eyes sparkling various shades of brown and her mouth, full pink lips, curled and slightly parted, revealing the slight overbite of her teeth and her tongue. She was beautiful and I swear, she was oblivious to it which only made her more attractive.

"Thank you." She looked across at the bed and the view before turning back to me. "You can take this room. I'll take one of the empty ones."

I shook my head. Her face when she'd spied the sea and blue skies from the terrace had made the decision of who was sleeping here. "You take this room, I'll take next door and maybe we could have a glass of something cold poolside, if you fancy it?"

"Yes, thanks. I'd like that."

By the time Madison came downstairs and outdoors, I had already prepared some dinner and opened a bottle of wine. She eyed it with slight suspicion but took my gesture towards an empty seat as the invitation I'd intended it to be.

"This looks nice." She looked down at the dinner of risotto and salad.

"Let's hope it tastes as good."

She took the glass of wine next to her plate and took a large gulp of it. She was nervous, and why wouldn't she be? I didn't think she had ever had an interaction with me that wasn't unpleasant and barbed.

We ate in relative silence and as we moved to sit on the comfy seats next to the fire pit that I lit, we both seemed a little more settled.

She was glorious at the best of times, but with the warm fire bathing her in its light, she was the most beautiful thing I had ever seen. I almost choked on my wine at that realisation, so set about distracting myself.

"I'm sorry that I didn't check on your relationship status before we embarked on this." I moved my finger between us before thinking I sounded a complete and utter twat. I didn't think I had ever uttered the words relationship status and I wasn't planning on doing it again any time soon.

She shook her head and uttered a small, single laugh. "Nor I yours."

I rolled my eyes at that. We both knew I had no relationship status.

"I'm single."

"Not any longer. You're married. We both are."

She nodded, realising her own error but not taking offence at my correction. Maybe we could survive the year without killing each other. "I was single."

I nodded, and then I remembered that she hadn't always been single. Dad had invited me to an engagement party for her, just before Helen died. I hadn't gone. It was nothing to do with me.

"What?" she asked. "You're frowning."

"Sorry. I thought you had been engaged, before . . ."

"I was, briefly. I thought he was the one I loved and wanted to be with, and he was for a time. Unfortunately, I wasn't the one he wanted to be with, well, not just me at least."

There was no bitterness or even anger in her words, just resignation.

"He cheated on you?" I waited for her reply, slightly disbelieving that anyone would want someone over Madison. I quickly shook that thought from my mind before I had to answer the questions in my head about why I held that belief when my treatment of her had always been in stark contrast to that.

Her reply was a single nod. "I think so. He never admitted it, but I think there was a crossover."

"I'm sorry he did that to you." I was. "For what it's worth, he was an idiot."

She looked shocked. "Water under the bridge and it was for the best. If he could have his head turned by someone else so easily then it was better that it happened sooner rather than later."

"I suppose, but I doubt I would be able to accept it with such dignity."

She made no response to my words but had clearly decided on a change of topic. "Right, let's top up these glasses and we can exchange favourite songs and movies."

BY THE FOLLOWING MORNING, AS I SET ABOUT FINDING some breakfast, I was more relaxed and although the thought of the next year was still on my mind, it wasn't weighing quite so heavily.

Last night had been relaxing and dare I say it, enjoyable, even with the conversation about the fiancé. We'd moved on from that and chatted and considering the fact we'd known each other for the last ten years, it was the first time we'd ever done that. Although, I had always made the effort to avoid her and had been openly hostile when we had been thrown together. We'd discussed music, films, books, everything aside from the fact that we were married. I'd seen a side to Madison I never had before. I knew that wasn't entirely true and it would have been more accurate to say that I'd seen a side to her I'd never wanted to see before. I had glimpsed it occasionally and immediately shut it down with an arsehole comment.

"Good morning."

I turned to find Madison standing behind me, already showered and dressed in a pair of denim cut-off shorts and a strapless top. Her face was free of any make-up and her hair hung around her shoulders in freshly washed, loose curls. She had looked beautiful as a bride, not that I'd found that a shock, she was an incredibly attractive woman, but today in a totally natural and effortless way she was sublime.

"Hi." A two-letter word and somehow, I had stammered over it.

She didn't seem to notice, or if she had, she hadn't shown it.

"Breakfast?" I was killing single word conversation this morning.

"Thank you. Can I help?" She was already pulling

juice from the fridge and preparing to make coffee and tea, presumably unsure which I would want.

That simple thing pulled me up short. Ten years we'd known each other, and she didn't know whether I drank orange or apple juice, tea, or coffee, not that I knew her any better, and yet here we were, married and with a challenge to convince the outside world this was real.

I stood in front of her, determined not to make this sound like I was being a dickhead. I wasn't, but we had both entered into this marriage with a lot to lose, so we needed to shift the odds in our favour.

"Shall we eat outdoors?" I was already piling fresh fruit into a bowl whilst waiting for my pan to heat for pancakes.

She nodded with a warm smile.

"And then we need to talk. I've been thinking."

"Careful." She laughed, the sound warming me. "Could be dangerous with your limited intelligence."

I scowled, ready to bite back, but when I turned, her face was full of good humour and friendly teasing, or at least it was until she saw my glowering expression.

Madison

AFTER LAST NIGHT, I WAS HOPING THAT WE MIGHT HAVE turned a corner and would be able to share a laugh, banter that didn't immediately turn into point scoring or an exchange of insults and barbed comments. Maybe not.

Last night, Gideon had been relaxed and in good spirits, even making awful jokes that made me laugh. Laughter he'd joined in with. We'd had a nice night, or so I'd thought. He'd seemed genuinely interested in what I had to say about everything, music, books, films, business even. That last fact had surprised me as I'd assumed there would only be one opinion he valued in business, his own, but I was wrong, and that fact thrilled me. I didn't dig any deeper on why that might be.

In business terms I was very much a novice. I worked for the publishing company my father had started from nothing, but that now was a Knight Inc. subsidiary. Gideon ran the whole thing. The big business and all of the smaller ones that formed part of the whole Knight empire. He had always worked for the family business as far as I could tell and since his father's retirement, he had taken the helm. He was renowned in business circles as being tough and uncompromising, but honest and fair. The business had never been a small fish, but with Gideon running things, it had become a whale!

As the business and the company name had developed and its reputation had grown, so had Gideon's, professionally and personally. He had become a firm favourite with the gossip columns and society pages alike. During his early twenties he had been the playboy in the latest bars and clubs, usually with at least one beautiful and scantily clad beauty on his arm. These were the locations of fights with paparazzi who loitered there and loved to provoke a rich playboy to lose his shit. Gideon rarely disappointed during these times. I couldn't remember the last time I'd seen or heard of him getting into a fight, but the paparazzi still loved him, chronicling every model, actress, and beautiful woman who undoubtedly passed through his bedroom. That thought made me shudder.

I brushed that aside and stared across at the surface of

the pool. Today I was going to swim a few lengths and soak up some sun here. I'd really enjoyed sitting here last night, eating dinner, and if I was honest, there were seconds where, albeit fleetingly, it felt as though we wanted to be there, together. The whole thing had felt easy and natural in a way it never had before.

When my mother had begun her affair with Gideon's dad, it had come as a surprise to me. She had been sad, and I assumed lonely and heartbroken when my father had died, we both had, but we had money and a home and each other, which helped. Then she had begun to smile and laugh a little more and that was because she had met Lucas.

Whilst Mum was a free agent, he wasn't. He told her his marriage was over and had been going through the motions for a number of years and when their affair had become more, when they had fallen in love, he had left his wife, divorced her, and married Mum. She was ecstatic to have the man she loved to herself, and he really did adore my mother. Me? It was odd to see her with another man, any man who wasn't my dad, and although I resented her ability to find happiness with another man, I didn't resent her. I had my own life to be getting on with and that is what I did, although I had only been eighteen at the time of their marriage.

Gideon? He was a different matter entirely. He had been furious that his mother had been left hurt and abandoned. For him, his parents' marriage had been perfect, and it was my mother who had come along and blown it out of the water. She had been the temptress and although his father hadn't resisted, he'd viewed him as being a pawn almost. Unfortunately, as much as he'd had a front row seat to his mother's heartbreak, he was privy to the same view of my mother's happiness. He never quite managed to separate the two and as such, his mother was the victim and mine was the villain.

When his open hostility to my mother reached its peak, I can only assume his father put his foot down very firmly when he married my mother because almost overnight, whilst still curt, his behaviour towards my mother changed, as did his treatment of me. Previously he had pretty much ignored my presence, with the odd barbed comment or sneer thrown in, but when my mother was removed from his aim, I became the figurehead for his hostility. He was unpleasant, laughed at me and made comments about everything from my personality to my appearance to my bloodline. Fortunately, from that point, our paths crossed less as I made my own life and avoided him when I could. After my mum died, that became easier as my relationship with Lucas became more distant, partly because he wasn't anything to me, not really, and also because my mum and I needed to deal with our own grief in our own way.

"Sorry."

I jumped at the sound of Gideon's apology.

"I know you were joking . . . it's just strange . . . this."

"Being together, being married, your father's plan?" I assumed it would be all of these facts that had caused his earlier scowl and change in mood.

"Yeah, they're all factors, but the strangest thing is discovering that I like you and that I had a very enjoyable evening with you."

I stared, my jaw slack at his words, not because I couldn't relate to what he was saying, perhaps because I could. I wasn't blind, never had been so had always recognised how attractive Gideon was. When I'd first met him and he hadn't been quite as unpleasant, I'd developed a crush I suppose, then quickly gone off him when he turned on me fully, but now, I liked him and enjoyed his company, and it was reciprocal. It looked as though the crush might be back.

Gideon

Fuck me! Why had I said that? I wanted to backtrack, but knew I wouldn't and when she nodded, well, I was speechless.

"Same and yes, it's strange."

I couldn't take my eyes off her lips as she spoke and all I could think about was what she would taste like if I kissed her. When I kissed her. This was not supposed to happen. I needed to get some space and regroup.

"I . . . erm, need to dress and I have to meet someone for lunch . . . a business associate." With that I was retreating before I said any more or leaned in and claimed her mouth as my own.

BLUE EYES THAT MATCHED MY OWN STARED BACK AT ME across the low table where tea and cake sat. Her eyes softened and twinkled, immediately putting me at my ease, eyes I suddenly realised were the only physical attribute

I'd inherited from my mother. Everything else had come from my dad.

"Let me clarify. I'd hate to have misunderstood anything." A sharp arch of her brow displayed more sarcasm than her tone ever could. "You have been manipulated into marrying Madison Forbes by your father. You have both consented to this and now you find yourself fighting the attraction to her because in spite of who she is and what she represents to you, you have always found her attractive?"

"I wouldn't have put it that way, Mother, but yes,"

She smirked at my use of mother, knowing that was my irked response.

"No? How would you have put it then?"

She had me over a barrel and she knew it.

"Okay, you may be fairly close to the mark," I conceded reluctantly.

Her eyebrow arching again was her only response.

"But what do I do? I thought it would be a year of tension and point scoring . . . mainly me point scoring," I admitted to her in a way I couldn't to anyone else.

"Oh, Gideon. I am bloody furious with your father for doing this. He knew this is how it would be for you, and can I say that you thinking a year of tension and point scoring was acceptable is anything but! However, your father has made this situation and you and Madison are going to have to deal with it."

"That's not especially helpful, Mum." I had no idea what would have been helpful in this hideous situation.

"I don't know what you want me to say. I could tell you to keep away from one another, to focus on the fact that her mother was the woman who had an affair with my husband and broke up my marriage, so shouldn't be trusted for a second."

I stared at her. She didn't sound bitter or angry, just indifferent. "Is that what you're saying?"

She laughed, startling me slightly. Reaching across, she took my hand in hers. "No, sweetheart, that is not what I am saying, and you know it. She is not her mother and shouldn't be punished for being her daughter any more than you should be punished for being your father's son, and this is not the first time I've told you this. Was I hurt by the affair? Of course, but I am over it. If everything had been rosy in the garden, she wouldn't have been able to steal him away from me, would she? Plus, she wasn't the one having the affair, he was, but I understand he was your father, your hero, so Helen bore the brunt of your anger, her and Madison."

"So?" I couldn't believe that I was here, at twenty-eight years old, asking my mum to sort out my problems for me.

"So, you get to sort this out yourself. You and Madison, but you might want to start seeing her as a person in her own right and remove your rose-tinted glasses where your father is concerned. He always was a manipulative and sneaky bastard in business, and now, even from beyond the grave, he is those things personally, too."

"Why don't you hate Helen?" Watching my mother speak about her husband's affair, the end of their marriage without bitterness and anger always shocked me, but I'd never asked her about it before.

She laughed and looked as beautiful as any woman I had ever seen.

"I did, for a while, but I quickly realised that it was

your father who'd betrayed me, and he did that because he fell in love. He hadn't loved me, or been in love with me for some time, and it was mutual. We both became indifferent to each other and our relationship, but we adored you." She brushed a hand, gently across my cheek. "Our little boy, the apple of both of our eyes, but it wasn't enough. I don't know if Helen was the first affair, but she was the first woman he loved after me and in a strange way, I was pleased for them. They both deserved to be happy, like we all do."

I was stunned into silence. She was amazing, the most amazing person I had ever met, and I had the privilege to call her my mother.

She laughed, presumably at my silence or my expression, maybe both.

"Gideon, I am sure this doesn't make sense to you. I'm not sure it makes sense to me, but maybe the tension and the point scoring you talked about is all you and Madison will have, but maybe your father saw something neither of us have."

My earlier silence morphed into a dumbfounded state that caused my mother to move until she sat next to me, an arm around my shoulders to pull me in close.

"Mum," was all I could manage to say.

"I know. Try to forget the arrangement, the business, Helen and your father, and maybe try to just see Madison."

I nodded, the power of speech still escaping me. I remained with my mother for the next couple of hours and left with a promise to meet up soon, for dinner, with Madison.

Madison

ONCE GIDEON HAD LEFT, I FELT A COMBINATION OF confusion and contentment. The reasons for my confusion were obvious, but the contentment rattled me slightly until I realised how tense I had been in his company, physically and emotionally. His presence had always made me tense, from the first day I met him, and that had never changed, not until last night. When we had sat together, talking, sharing a bottle of wine, the tension had lifted. I was unsure if I had realised that until it had returned that morning, but I knew for sure it hadn't been present last night, nor this morning until his weird mood change.

When he had apologised and tried to explain his behaviour, I was sure he was going to kiss me. The way he seemed unable to stop looking at my lips, and the truth was, I was disappointed when he didn't.

Gideon had always been attractive, or at least I had always found him to be. He had been a slightly gangly seventeen-year-old when I'd first met him at sixteen. He'd initially been indifferent to me. Ignoring my presence, but that quickly changed. My mother had gone from being the other woman to the girlfriend and whilst I hadn't been thrilled to be living with her and Lucas in a new home, I had no choice at that point, unlike Gideon. He lived with his mother in his family home and when visiting his father was forced to spend time with the woman who had, in his mind, wrecked his parent's marriage. During those visits he extended his hostility to me. After my mother died, I had spent time with Lucas who had been clear that my mother had never been a fling. He had loved her, he said from the second he'd set eyes on her. I assumed he had never told his son that, or more likely, his son refused to believe it.

Lying on a lounger next to the pool, I rolled over to get some sun on my back and flicked the clasp on my bikini to avoid *white bits* and thought back to that first meeting. Gideon had been openly hostile to my mother. We were of a similar age and as such, I'd hoped we might get on. Ultimately, we didn't. Or at least *he* didn't. Once he had turned on me, he shut me down every time I attempted to speak to him and when I spoke to anyone else, he scoffed and made fun of everything I said. I had found him gorgeous and as such that made me slightly uncomfortable and a little bumbling and his attitude towards me made those things worse.

From that point on, every time our paths crossed, his behaviour became worse. I just wanted him to like me and didn't understand why he despised me. It took me years to make any sense of it. By the time my mother died, he'd reluctantly accepted her place in his father's life, and I was resigned to the fact that he was a complete and utter twat and no longer craved his approval. We had a relationship based on mutual loathing, or so I thought until we got married! I still couldn't believe Lucas had done that to us.

Gideon had fully taken over his family business when his father retired after my mother's death. I had gone straight from university into my father's business that my mother owned and made my way through the ranks. When my mother died, it had been assumed that the business would go straight to me. It hadn't. She had left everything other than some personal effects to her husband and although he had allowed me to work for the business and help to run it, it was still his. Again, the assumption was made by everyone else that upon his death, the business would be mine and his own business would go to Gideon. I laughed out loud at the thought of that because if he'd done what was expected, neither I nor Gideon would be in this ridiculous position now. With hindsight, Lucas had never said my father's business would come to me. He'd inferred it, but no more. And now, here we were, married, confused and no longer indifferent or hating each other.

Chapter Five

Gideon

Silence greeted me as I entered the villa. Moving through the living area and the kitchen, I could see the glass doors to the back of the house were open and the pool glistened beyond. I made my way towards the doors but still heard nothing. Just as I was about to call out to Madison, I saw her, possibly asleep. She was lying on her front, topless, soaking up the sunshine and she was a bloody vision.

I was unsure if it was sun lotion, sweat or water from the pool, but her whole body shimmered, and there was a lot of skin on show. She wore white bikini bottoms and that was all. I could see the straps of the top hanging loosely at the side of the lounger she lay on. Her hair was piled on her head leaving her neck and shoulders exposed. Unable to do anything else, I moved closer, then closer still until I stood next to her. Crouching, my face was almost at the same level as hers, her eyes closed. I blew on her cheek, not wanting to startle her.

The plan to not startle her didn't quite work out when my gentle blow saw her eyes fly open at that exact second;

she sprung up until she was kneeling on the lounger staring at me, one earphone bud being pulled out. So, she wasn't asleep but listening to music.

"Sorry," I began and then as I took in her heavy breathing, my gaze dropped and I saw she was virtually naked before me and looked like heaven on earth.

She followed my eyes and immediately began to cover herself with her hands and then a nearby towel. "You nearly gave me a heart attack, Gideon." She pulled the other bud from her ear. "Do we have a clause for killing each other in our marriage?" Her question came with a half laugh that I joined in with until my eyes fixed on hers.

"You're beautiful," I told her, unsure what else to say. Recalling my mother's words about just seeing Madison suddenly made sense.

"Thank you."

She looked awkward now. More awkward than when I had been staring at her tits. Strange. "I'm sorry." There was uncertainty in my voice as I wondered just what I was sorry for and my own doubts over the reason for my apology was mirrored by her expression. "I don't know what for, beyond this whole debacle my father has forced us into."

She stared at me, but said nothing, unlike me.

"And for treating you so badly." Clearly, I was getting some clarity on the reason for my apology.

She found her voice again. "I'm not sure I can hold you responsible for your father's will."

She'd misunderstood.

"That's not what I meant. For everything. From the first time I met you, my treatment of your mother and then you, and for everything since. I was rude, hostile, and made you the figurehead of my anger and sadness at my parents' marriage ending."

"Maybe because it was my mother–"

Fuck me! If she wasn't making excuses for me. Excuses I didn't deserve. Yet again, my mother's voice was in my head. "No, please. Your mother bore some responsibility, maybe my mother played a part too, but my dad was the one entirely in the wrong, never you. Forgive me, please." The pleading in my voice shocked me, but in that specific second, there was nothing I wanted more than her forgiveness.

She smiled. "How about a clean slate?"

"Thank you, I'd like that."

She extended a hand and offered me the warmest of grins. "Hi, I'm Madison Forbes, you must be Gideon. Very pleased to meet you."

"The pleasure is all mine." I accepted her hand and kissed the back of it and felt as though an explosion had gone off in my mind. Nothing had ever felt so good or so natural as my lips on her skin.

She pulled her hand back quickly and when I returned my gaze to her face, she was more flushed and breathing heavier than when I'd almost given her a heart attack by blowing on her face. Her eyes were alight with something. Surprise? No. Desire. She wanted me and by fuck if I didn't want her too. Reaching forward, acting on instinct alone, I cupped her face and pulled her to me, the towel dropping away as I lowered my lips to hers and kissed her as her arms wrapped around my neck, pulling me in and holding me close as her mouth greedily accepted mine.

Madison

WHAT THE HELL WAS HAPPENING? I MEAN, I KNEW THE immediate answer to that was that Gideon was kissing me, although, that was a very inadequate description. No kiss had ever felt like this, ever. He was going to ruin me for anyone else because I'd never be able to go back to kisses less than this.

Eventually, he pulled back slightly and looked down at me with a very sexy, easy smile.

"What are you thinking?" I asked, unsure where we went from here. I knew where I'd like it to go but I was unsure whether that was my mind, heart or lady parts talking.

"Honestly? I am wondering if the rest of your body will taste as divine as your mouth. What are you thinking?"

"That your kiss has ruined me for any other man."

Looking at his eyes darkening and closing slightly, I wondered if I had said the wrong thing. The little growl that sounded in the back of his throat while he pulled me to him until he was picking me up, the cheeks of my arse filling his hands, suggested my words had been anything but wrong.

"You have no need to worry about any other man's kisses. You're mine now."

His lips crashed back to mine as he carried me into the house, bypassing every room until we reached the end of the corridor where our neighbouring rooms met.

"Your room or mine?" I gave him the choice but didn't care which one he chose. I just wanted him to choose one quickly.

He shook his head. "No such thing anymore. Our room."

The door to the master suite was already opening behind me and I was being carried in and deposited in the middle of the bed.

Lying there I looked up and was shocked at just how handsome Gideon was. It wasn't like I hadn't appreciated how attractive he was before, I had, but now, with his eyes ablaze with desire fixed firmly on me, standing over me, his breathing heavy, he was so much more than attractive. Grabbing the hem of his pristine white t-shirt it quickly flew across the room leaving his hands dropping to the button of his shorts that were soon being pushed down, revealing his naked erection beneath them.

Subconsciously, I licked my lips. A quirk of his eyebrows and a cocky smirk was his response as he knelt on the bed and then he was blanketing me, nothing between us as he kissed me again.

His lips traced a path down my body, like the gentlest of breezes dancing across my skin until I was a mass of sensation and goosebumps. Moans escaped from my lips as I craved more from him whilst at the same time wanting less.

Suddenly, he stopped, and I felt bereavement followed by panic. What if he had changed his mind about this? About me? Glancing down I found him kneeling at the side of the bed, his face between my splayed thighs. Slowly, he picked up one of my feet and kissed the instep then proceeded to kiss his way up higher until I could feel his warm breath cooling against my most intimate folds.

My moan was almost deafening.

"My wife likes my plan then?"

He had never called me his wife before, not like this, but that is exactly who and what I was. *His* wife. He licked along my drenched length, and I swear, I was soaring, almost coming on the spot. My gasps and garbled cries continued as he maintained his gloriously torturous assault on my body. His body pressed between my thighs, prevented the instinctive closing of my legs, not that I wanted to really stop this. I was edging closer and closer to the precipice of a cliff, teetering on the verge of pleasure and release. I knew it wouldn't take much more, maybe just one more touch, and how he delivered it. Two fingers slid inside me, immediately turning and curling against that sensitive button deep within me. I drew in a breath, tightening every muscle in my body until there was nowhere else for me to go other than into the spiral of release. Just when I thought he couldn't make this any better or extend and intensify the sweet bliss uncoiling within me, he drew my clit into the hot heat of his mouth and sucked on it.

Reaching down, I grabbed for him, only managing to find his hair. My fingers laced through the thick strands and pulled him in, refusing to let him withdraw, scared that this pleasure might end. More scared that once it ended, these feelings and sensations might never be rediscovered.

Large hands covered my smaller ones and prised them away. With my hands still in his, he looked up, his face glistening with my arousal. It was his turn to lick his lips now. With a huge grin still in place he made his way back up my body until we were face to face, his lips almost against mine, close enough that I could feel his breath and smell my own aroma.

"I knew you'd taste divine."

I felt heat warm my cheeks as I flushed.

"And I don't think I will ever get enough of it, or making you come. Are you sure?"

As if I was going to change my mind about this when he had the ability to make me feel as amazing as he just had.

"I'm sure."

"Good, because I'm ready to explode. I should have asked, not that we exactly planned this, but contraception . . ."

Clearly, this was all a little backwards to be having this discussion naked with me barely recovered from a breath-taking orgasm I might never recover from.

"I'm protected and I haven't been with anyone for a while," I admitted, unsure why I felt a little awkward to be admitting the last part.

By contrast, Gideon looked thrilled by my revelation. "A while?"

"Yes, two years,"

His grinned broadened. "Two years?"

"Closer to three."

"You need to stop speaking or I am going to embarrass myself badly."

I giggled. "That would be such a shame."

"Agreed, so . . ."

He was poised at my entrance and just as I thought he was ready to enter me, he paused, as if seeking final permission.

"Gideon, do *I* need you to use a condom?"

In that second the atmosphere changed and turned serious. This was real and there would be no going back from it, certainly not for me, but I suspected for him, too.

"I'm clean, completely."

"Should I ask how long it's been for you?" Why had I asked that question? Did I want the answer to it?

"You can ask me anything and I will answer you honestly."

The sincerity in his voice and his pledge humbled me somehow and I absolutely believed what he was saying.

"So, do you have anything else to say, to ask?"

I reached up and pulled his lips to mine while I wrapped my legs around his behind and used my feet to urge him to continue.

Chapter Six

Gideon

The sensation of sliding inside her was sublime and like nothing I had ever known. This was so much more than I thought it might be. From the second our lips had touched it had promised so much and it had certainly delivered. When people used words like electrifying, an explosion or intensity in relation to sex, I'd got it, or at least I thought I had, and then I touched Madison and I realised I never had before. This was all of those things and more. I was on fucking fire, inside and out and before this had even ended, I was craving more of it, of her.

The sounds she made in an aroused state were enough to bring me to my knees, the mewls, moans and little rumbling sounds, but fuck me, if the sight of her absorbing her own pleasure, the contradictive movements of pulling me closer and yet pushing me away, they might be my undoing. I couldn't even begin to describe how she tasted. She was like nothing I had ever known. I was struggling to correlate the woman beneath me, positively glowing as we became one, to the person I had met all those years ago.

The same one I had been nothing but hostile to. Maybe if I hadn't been such a young, arrogant, and angry prick, we may have got here sooner, or maybe we were meant to wait for it. My mother's words about my father seeing something we hadn't, came rushing to the forefront of my mind as Madison began to tighten around my hard length that was thrusting a little faster now. She was going to come again and this time, it really would see me coming undone too. I had been dangerously close to it when she'd come on my tongue.

"Gideon," she called, pulling my attention back to her completely. Her hands cradled my face while her lips curled into the sexiest of smiles and her legs that were wrapped around me, her feet on my behind, pulled me in closer.

"Fuck," I cried, feeling my balls begin to tighten as my arousal threatened to pass the point of no return. "You are beautiful." I hadn't planned on saying that but looking down at her, seeing the glow of arousal shining from her eyes, hearing the huskiness of her voice as she too edged closer to release and not least the sensation of her body, drawing me in, possessing and owning me seemed to scramble my mind so that I simply acted on impulse.

Her breathing hitched causing a frown to crease her brow. "I'm going to come."

"Do it, baby, for me, with me." I grunted, increasing my pace, needing to see her in all her glory and share the moment with her.

She pulled my lips to hers once more and kissed me, slightly frantically as her pleasure soared, preparing for the fall once it reached its peak. While she may have started the kiss, I was determined to finish it. One hand fisted in her hair and the other slid beneath her behind, pulling her closer so I could really increase my speed as I thrust inside her, brushing against her clit with every move. I traced kisses from her mouth along her jaw until my lips rested at her ear.

"Come on. Come for me, come all over me as I fuck you." I had no idea if she needed or wanted my dirty words, but she got them anyway and I hoped they didn't ruin the moment for her.

"Yes, fuck me!" she cried as her hands that were on my back and shoulders began to claw at the skin there.

Clearly, my dirty words were not a problem.

"I'm going to come, baby. Can you feel how hard you make me?"

"Yes," she moaned, her nails possibly breaking the skin on my back, but it only added to the moment.

"You like me fucking you, don't you? It makes you hot and wet, doesn't it?"

"Yes, Gideon, please, make me come for you."

That was my undoing, the pleading and near request for permission to come, not that I thought she'd be in any position to stop even if I denied her. One final thrust as my face nestled into her neck, absorbing the scent and taste of the skin there saw her coming, calling my name, holding me close and wrapping everything around me. Her internal muscles were flexing and tensing, having the workout of their life. Together with the woman herself and her pleasure, they took me there with her, groaning through gritted teeth as my hand tightened on her arse, possibly leaving my mark there. I briefly registered a shocked cry from Madison when my mouth that had been in her neck moved to her shoulder and subconsciously bit into her flesh, but it was quickly replaced with a moan of pleasure, as together we rode out the remnants of our releases.

Madison

LYING TOGETHER IN BED SEEMED THE MOST NATURAL thing in the world and the most alien. Here, wrapped within the warm embrace of Gideon's arms and legs felt like home. He ran his fingers up and down the length of my arm, not quite tickling me, but sensitizing the skin enough that the hairs on my whole body stood on end as I shivered and shuddered.

"Cold?" he asked, pulling my back closer to his front whilst pulling the sheet over us both.

"No, you're giving me the shivers."

His whole body stiffened against me. "Shivers? Do you want me to stop, or leave, or . . ." His voice trailed off.

With his grip on me having loosened, I was able to turn in his arms and face him. He looked wary, nervous even.

"No." I was already pulling his hand back to my arm, silently confirming my word and asking him to continue. "They were good shivers."

"Good shivers?" He smiled.

"Yeah, good shivers. I like your hands on me."

His smile morphed into a grin. "Good job because I plan on having them all over you, inside and out."

My eyes dropped and I swear my face glowed with the heat of an embarrassed flush making him laugh.

"How about we take a swim and soak up some sun this afternoon?"

"I'd like that." I looked up to find his gaze fixed firmly

on my face. "Although, I began that plan before you interrupted my sun worshipping with your slightly psychotic, serial killer creeping up and blowing on me routine."

He laughed, a proper chuckle that sounded as though he was completely and utterly happy and at peace.

"I was trying not to startle you." He still laughed as he offered a defence if that's what his words were.

"Ha! And how did that work out for you?"

"Honestly? Pretty fucking marvellously as it led to us being in bed together."

His laughter had gone, his expression had darkened, and his jaw was set giving him a deadly serious look. I felt unsure if I needed to say anything in response. Him continuing to speak confirmed that I didn't.

"It led to me kissing you, carrying you up here, laying you down on our bed, kissing and tasting you everywhere until you came on my tongue, crying and moaning my name, and finally to me being inside you, fucking you until we both came. So, blowing on your face may have been the best decision I ever made."

I stared at him, speechless and slightly emotional, and although I could feel my desire rising at his words and the feel and sight of the gorgeous specimen before me, his less than romantic words, I felt moved by them.

"The swimming and soaking up the sun might have to wait." His hands were already reaching for me, his thumbs brushing across my cheeks as he drew me closer, preparing to kiss me.

"Wait?"

"Yes. Wait. I need you, my beautiful wife."

Chapter Seven

Gideon

Sitting around the conference room table, listening to all of the voices drone on allowed me to zone out slightly. I sometimes did that, safe in the knowledge that no significant decisions could be made without me rubberstamping them. Since returning from honeymoon a couple of months before, I'd done it more frequently and my thoughts always made their way to Madison, my wife.

My wife. That always brought a strange smile to my face. Thoughts of her made me smile. We were happy. From the second we'd given in to our attraction at the poolside, it had been that way, not that we didn't still find that friction that had been between us for so long, we did. The difference now was that we had so much more than that. We argued about things, of course we did, but we always made up and there were times when I thought it was worth the fight in order to do the making up.

When we'd first returned from honeymoon, Madison had dragged her heels a little on moving her stuff into my father's house. I had been a bit of an arsehole about it in the end and reminded her of the agreement she'd be in breach of if she didn't. I felt guilty about that now. Eventually, after several days of fighting, she broke down and admitted that the house had bad memories for her. She had lived there for a time, something I had never done, and although she'd moved out before her mother's death, she had moved back in when Helen had become very unwell and had helped care for her until she died. Her mother had died in that house, and I hadn't even thought about that fact until she broke down before me. If I could have changed where we lived, I would have, but I couldn't because those were the terms of my father's will. What I had done though, was to ensure that some changes were made to the house and we also stayed in my apartment a few nights each week.

Our current disagreement was about her name. In work she was known as Madison Forbes and had insisted on remaining that way. I had told her from the first day, after the wedding that she would be changing it. She had dug her heels in, but then so had I, so, when she suggested becoming Madison Forbes-Knight, I had shut it down. This had been rolling on since we'd said I do which was far too long for me and now we were currently at a stalemate, kind of.

My current thoughts shifted to images of our shower sex that morning. It wasn't make up sex as such because our issue was ongoing, for now.

Madison was glorious in every way, but wet and wanton, desperate for what only I gave her, she was intoxicating. That morning, she had woken before me and was already in the shower when I entered the bathroom. Seconds barely passed before I was in the enclosure with her, my mouth on hers and our hands exploring each other. The memory of her being pressed against the wall, her arms holding me tight, her legs wrapped around me as I entered her caused my cock to harden. The sound of her gasps and moans were captured by our kiss. Fuck! I needed her like I needed my next breath and the aching in my groin confirmed that. What were the chances of me being able to pay her a visit this afternoon? Maybe we could have a lunch date with each other being on the menu.

I came back to the present with a start as the sound of the door flying open coincided with my wife storming in, followed by one of the panic-struck receptionists, apologising. Whatever conversations had been in place around the table came to an abrupt end as did my dreams of some one on one time with her. All eyes turned to a furious Madison.

"How dare you!" She roared, oblivious to her surroundings and everyone present except me. "We talked about this, argued about this, and I thought we were still discussing it to find a compromise, but no! You have taken the decision into your own hands and simply done as you wanted. You arrogant, ars—"

I cut her off. "Stop!" She did, although I was in no doubt that my interruption and one word barked command would come back and bite me at some point. That could wait because this conversation needed to be private and definitely not shared with my employees who were all agog, their gazes flitting between me and her like they were watching a game of bloody tennis. "We'll reconvene at four," I told them all before turning to the flustered receptionist who was still muttering her apologies. "It's fine, thank you, my wife is not someone to be stopped, except by me."

I couldn't resist that last comment, for those present, but mainly for Madison herself who shot me a death-defying glare now.

Everyone left quickly and for a few seconds, silence hung between us, thick, heavy and loaded.

"Can I get you a drink?" I was unsure why I was extending social niceties like the offer of a drink. Maybe I was hoping to diffuse the angst and tension that had put a wedge between us.

She shook her head. Maybe the diffusion tactic was working. "I'd much rather you told me what the fuck you thought you were doing and why you value my thoughts and independence so little."

Looked like angst was back, but my reaction was anything but. I felt hurt by her suggestion.

"I value everything about you." She was close enough to touch, and cupping her face in my hands, I dropped my head to hers. "Very, very highly." My lips were preparing to cover hers, but then she spoke again.

"Not from where I am standing because if you did, my offices and every piece of signage and official stationery would not now be plastered with the name Madison Knight, would it?" Disentangling herself from me, she stepped back.

I considered trying to play this off as being something I had done out of kindness or even as a grand romantic gesture, but neither were true, and we both knew it.

"You are Madison Knight. That is a fact."

"And you are an arsehole!" she spat.

"Yes, the arsehole you married." This was going badly,

and I could already feel that we might both say things we wouldn't be able to take back.

"And the same arsehole I'll be divorcing!"

There it was. The elephant in the room. The words that couldn't be taken back. The same words that silenced us both, reminding us of the fact that this wasn't real. The breakfasts and dinners we shared, the lounging on the sofa in front of the TV sharing a bottle of wine, the dates and functions we attended and the sex. None of it was real. It was all fake. We were playing house for one reason and one reason only. Money. I felt embarrassed by that fact, but that wasn't the emotion that shocked and scared me most, that honour belonged to hurt. I was reeling at her words, but it was the reality behind them. Not the arsehole, that was par for the course with us and there were times when she made it sound like a term of endearment, but the divorce. She intended to divorce me and that hurt me, hurt and saddened me.

I didn't want us to divorce. I wanted to be married to her. I wanted to keep her as my wife. Fuck! I loved her.

Madison

"WHY ARE YOU MAKING THIS EVEN MORE COMPLICATED?" Josie filled up our glasses and stared across the table at me.

Rather than look directly at her, I scanned the restaurant we were in and could see nothing but happy couples enjoying each other's company at lunch. People in love or at least open to the possibility of it. I wondered what Gideon and I had looked like to the outside world when we went on dates together. Did we look at each other like the couple next to me and Josie. Maybe not. They clearly adored each other, and I doubted the reason they were together was because of money or clauses in wills.

The click of my friend's fingers in front of my face saw me jumping and instinctively batting her hand away.

"Don't bloody click at me!" I snapped.

She arched a brow in surprise, or possibly a silent reprimand. "Then don't ignore me. You are the one who has been miserable for weeks and I am the one who has been your sounding board and stood by your side."

"Sorry."

She nodded her acceptance of my apology.

"I haven't been miserable."

She arched her brows and shook her head slightly but remained silent.

"I haven't. Confused maybe."

"Okay." She drew the word out and I wasn't sure if she'd been aiming for disbelief or simple questioning.

"I haven't," I repeated. "I'm just confused."

"Explain."

And I did. I told her about the Gideon I had been privy to. The man who made me breakfast in bed at weekends and sent me to work with a packed lunch. The same man who held doors open for me and rebuked anyone who didn't say please and thank you in their dealings with me. I admitted he was the one who took my breath away with a touch or a glance, and also, finally admitted that we had been having sex and every time got better than the last. She didn't look entirely surprised by that.

"Sounds perfect."

She was right. It did. But she was forgetting one simple fact.

"But it isn't real and is entirely temporary." Admitting that, hearing the words out loud hurt me. The burn in my jaw and the sting of tears welling in my eyes, whilst unexpected had been a long time coming really.

"Babe," she said, taking my hand in hers. "It's only temporary if you want it to be, and you clearly don't."

"Me wanting it isn't enough. He has to want it too."

She nodded. "Who says he doesn't?"

"This is Gideon Knight we are talking about. He doesn't do commitment or anything beyond a fling and his priorities are and always have been, business."

"Is this why the name thing is a sticking point for you?"

I frowned. I didn't understand what my friend was asking. Keeping my name was important for many reasons. It was all I had left of my dad and the divorce, when it came, would be bad enough without me having to revert to my former name as well as my former life.

"When, if I take a man's name it will be because I intend to keep it."

"You old romantic." Josie wasn't making fun or teasing. No, her voice carried nothing but empathy for my situation. "You have to talk to him, and not just about the name because whatever the two of you have between you may have started as business but those pesky feelings appear to have put in an appearance."

She was right on the feelings front, well, for me at least. I had never had a one-night-stand, nor a casual relationship. By the time I slept with a man there had always been feelings and now, Gideon was no different. I liked him. Cared for him. Loved him. Shit! This had never been in my plan and now as well as losing my name, I was going to end up with a broken heart too.

Josie looked at her watch, something she'd done several times already meaning she was late or needed to go.

"Thanks, for this," I told her. "If you need to get off . . ."

"If you need me, I can stay a little longer."

I smiled at her generous offer, but there was no more to be said. "No. I'm fine. I might have a coffee or something then I'll go back to the office for a while before I head home and try to reason with Gideon about my name."

She laughed and I joined in, not that I thought reasoning was in Gideon's repertoire.

∾

Arriving home, I was surprised to find Gideon already there and in the kitchen preparing dinner.

"Hi," I said, slightly nervous of his reaction after the way we'd parted earlier.

"Hi." He smiled.

"What's for dinner?"

"Stir fry, if that's okay for you?" Gideon looked between the vegetables he was chopping and me.

I didn't have much of an appetite since my stomach was in knots at the anticipation of the conversation we needed to have and my reluctance to enter into another heated argument but he was making an effort. "Stir fry sounds good." Closing the distance between us, I moved until my front rested against his back and my arms closed around his middle. If only everything could stay as simple as when we were like this, just the two of us.

"Hey." He pulled my clasped arms apart and throwing the knife onto the countertop, he spun, cupping my face as he gazed down into my eyes. "You okay?"

"Sorry," we said in stereo making each other laugh.

"After you," Gideon almost bowed in my direction.

"Sorry for shouting and bursting into your office earlier."

"Accepted, but if I hadn't done the name change thing without telling you first, you wouldn't have needed to, so, I am sorry too."

I noticed his choice of word *without **telling** you first*, not ***asking.***

Neither of us said anything else until we'd sat down to eat dinner together.

"Can we discuss my name?"

I watched him stiffen which told me he didn't want to. As far as he was concerned there was nothing to discuss.

"We can, but let's be real here. It's done. You are Madison Knight. The world knows you're Madison Knight and now the business literature reflects that."

"Doesn't sound as though we have anything left to discuss on it then, does it?"

He ran a hand through his hair and then pressed two fingers to each of his temples and screwed his eyes shut as if in pain. "What do you want me to say? What message will that send to the rest of the world and specifically the business world if I change it back?"

"I don't care what it says to them."

He got to his feet, the sound of the chair scraping across the floor as it was pushed back, and then he fixed me with an expression I hadn't seen for a while. Hostility. Doesn't give a shit about me Gideon was back.

"Yeah, well maybe you should because it will look as though this is a marriage of convenience. A sham. Maybe even one that only has financial gain attached to it, and if that becomes common opinion, we both lose everything."

"Gideon . . ." I had no clue what words were going to follow, but as my voice trailed off, his kicked in.

"Madison, no. Suck it up!" He stormed across the room and after grabbing his jacket was heading for the door.

Standing, I called him back, my voice shaking with emotion and the first of my tears ready to breach the dam of my eyes. He turned.

"You asked what the rest of the world would think if you changed my name back," I let out a single hard and hollow laugh. "What you really should have asked is what *I* would think if you didn't."

He seemed to falter for a second, but he quickly recovered. "I'm going out. Don't wait up, darling."

As the door slammed, I dropped to the floor and sobbed. My feelings for him were clearly not reciprocated because if they were, he would have at least discussed this tonight and sought a compromise with me. He didn't. He'd simply walked out and left me.

Chapter Eight

Gideon

She was the mind fuck to end all mind fucks, her and these ridiculous feelings I had developed for her. I loved her. I wanted her to have my name and yet, that was the last thing she wanted. She wanted to keep her name and her business and end our arrangement at the earliest opportunity, that much was clear, even to me in my current drunken state.

I had no idea how I had ended up here, in a very high-end strip joint. That wasn't true. I knew how I had physically gotten here, that wasn't what I meant. After Madison left my office, I had taken some calls, completed some work, and then I'd gone home with a plan to cook dinner, and hopefully resolve things. I didn't want to scare her off by declaring love, but I thought we might manage to look at how things were between us and acknowledge that our marriage wasn't the business transaction we had originally imagined it would be.

When Madison had asked to talk, I was hopeful, but as her sole focus had been her name, it was already on shaky ground. I should have deflected attention from that topic until we'd talked about the change between us and possibly introduced the idea of feelings developing. Clearly, the feelings were very much one-sided and all from my end.

"Hey, what the fuck are you doing here?" Simon dropped down in the seat next to me.

"What the fuck am I doing here? What the fuck are *you* doing here?" I had come here alone and hadn't contacted Simon.

"Someone spotted you, so I came to check on you."

I laughed, scoffing at his words and their sentiment. "Are you staging an intervention?"

He shook his head. "Depends. Do I need to?"

Did he? I had no idea if he did or not.

"This is a very risky move on your part. Being here, being drunk. The paps outside are going to have a field day to find recently married and reformed confirmed bachelor, playboy, Gideon Knight kicking back, pissed in a strip joint."

"The paps can fuck off!" Not mature but it was all I had.

"They will enjoy even more, the failing of your marriage in under a year and you and your wife losing everything. Now pull yourself together and let's go."

"My wife!" I shouted and drew the attention of a few people nearby. The stripper on stage winked at me and I couldn't deny I was tempted. Right up to the point where Simon was in my line of sight, standing between me and her.

"Not a fucking chance! You agreed to this ridiculous plan cooked up by your old man, you and Madison. I told you to contest and by God you would have won, but you wanted to maintain his reputation which whilst admirable was stupid, but you made this situation. Now, let's go before you fuck it all up."

I staggered to my feet, ready to fight my friend. "I've already fucked it up. Madison is everything. She is beautiful and smart. A pain in the arse, sarky and snarky and gets under my skin like nobody ever has and now, to top it all . . ." I laughed, loudly and wobbled a little. "I love her. I fucking love my wife, even when I'd like to throttle her!"

The act on the stage had just ended and my declaration of love and possible murder was delivered to a near silent room. I held their rapt attention, much to Simon's horror judging by his muttered curses.

"What?" I addressed the whole room. "You think I'm mad to love my wife and be driven to the edge of insanity by her, don't you?"

A few people turned away; some ignored my show while others continued to observe. An older man was walking towards me and smiled.

"Gideon Knight. I knew your father, Nathanial Marks," he said and I as I clumsily accepted the hand he offered, panicked that he knew my marriage was a sham. "Congratulations on the wedding, the wife and the long marriage ahead."

Was this fucker being sarcastic? I couldn't tell because his words sounded sincere.

He laughed, possibly sensing my confusion. "The insanity thing, wanting to throttle her, and I am guessing never being sure whether you should fuck her or divorce her?"

I nodded and heard Simon mutter again about us being screwed.

Nathanial continued. "That's the perfect recipe for a long marriage. I'm thirty years into mine and at the risk of sounding like a masochist, I have never been happy, but if she doesn't know you're here, you might want to calm yourself down a little or she'll know before you turn your key in the door tonight." He turned to Simon. "You're the cavalry? Anything I can do?"

"No, we're good, thanks."

Nathanial was wrong, maybe not about him and his wife, but then I doubted they'd been coerced into a marriage of convenience. I was heading for the door with Simon who was suddenly acting as drunk as me and hadn't had a drink.

"What are you doing?"

"Saving your arse and possibly your marriage. This way, I will be the wanker who stropped off to a strip club and got drunk, and you can be the hero who joined me, got drunk with me and then got me home safely."

"Oh."

"The word you're looking for is thanks, and you are welcome, but you owe me one."

"I do. Thanks."

The door opened and the flash of lights going off was blinding. Shit! There was no way Madison would be able to remain oblivious to this even if she lived under a rock. I just hoped she didn't think I'd cheated on her. I hadn't. I wouldn't and it had nothing to do with losing my business and everything to do with losing her.

Madison

My phone rang with an unknown number. Usually I ignored those, but tonight, I didn't. Maybe because I was distracted by the way Gideon had walked out and the clear realisation that the feelings I had for him were in no way reciprocated.

He'd already been gone for hours, and I was still downstairs, sitting in the lounge with a glass of juice, refusing to trade it for alcohol, in fear of it making me melancholy. I had tried to drink away the loss of each of my parents, even though I was probably too young to drink when my father had died. It had been a bad plan and the addition of alcohol only ever made my pain even more unbearable.

Connecting the call, I recognised the voice immediately, Maria Ferguson.

"Mrs. Knight, Madison, how are you? It's Maria Ferguson."

What the fuck did she want? "I'm fine, or I was until my night was interrupted."

She laughed. This woman had no shame. It was almost eleven o'clock at night. There was no good reason for her calling and at that second, I hated Gideon for inviting her into our lives.

"Apologies."

Had a single word ever been more insincere? I doubted it.

"I just wanted a quote from you, about Gideon, your husband, your marriage."

I shook my head, hoping to clarify for myself what the hell she was talking about.

"I don't understand."

"Oh, sorry, a moment."

The phone went silent and then my own phone chimed into life with image after image of Gideon . . . entering a strip club alone, images of him inside, drinking, eyeing up the strippers, there was one of him folding a handful of notes while a stripper in a bikini top and a barely there thong stood over him. Bastard! This was obviously how he reacted to crossed words, or me attempting to stand up for myself. How dare he! I didn't even care that he was in breach of our marriage contract from Lucas' will. I was reeling from just how hurt I was. I hadn't been this hurt when my fiancé had actually cheated on me and that man I had loved, thought I had and had been planning to marry him for real.

Shit! The man I had married by arrangement meant more to me than one I had voluntarily entered into an engagement with, and the former was breaking my heart by not loving me back.

I continued to look through the pictures and saw Gideon speaking with a man, Nathanial Marks. He owned a huge publishing company I had once applied to do my internship with. I now noticed Simon was there too. The final images were of Simon and Gideon leaving the club, dozens of images being taken by paps I imagined and then they all but fell into the back of a cab.

Maria's voice was back. "The stripper . . . she will be giving me an exclusive on the private show she put on for your *husband*."

Her emphasis on the word husband made me want to slap her, curl up in a ball and hurt Gideon. I did none of those.

"No comment."

I couldn't quite believe that he had done this to me or himself. I knew this wasn't the fairy tale happy ending others may have imagined it to be, but fuck me, one real difference of opinion, one bone of contention and as soon as I had stood up to him, he had gone and found himself a stripper to do Lord knows what to. Why had I ever dreamed that this might work out or that Gideon was capable of giving me any more than his hostility. The reality was that no matter how good the sex was, how far I may have thought our relationship had come or could have grown, he clearly despised me. Far more than I had ever given him credit for.

Without any conscious thought I had moved upstairs and was quickly throwing some basic belongings into a bag.

I was leaving him, and it was no more than he deserved. I had too much self-respect to put up with his utter lack of it and total disregard for me as a human being never mind as his wife. The thought of losing my father's business upset me, but I knew I was worth more than what he was giving me. He could have it all because no matter what his wealth amounted to, in my mind he was a pauper emotionally.

Thank fuck I never declared my love for him as that really would have added insult to injury. Me knowing that he knew I loved him and that even my love wasn't enough.

The tears streamed down my face, and I did nothing to stop them. The sooner these feelings and emotions left my body, the sooner I could get on with my life and forget the name Gideon Knight forever. I wasn't even convincing myself that was possible. He owned me in the most basic of ways, but if no other person ever brought me to this low that he had, I could live with them never giving me the high.

Chapter Nine

Gideon

I was drunk, there was no denying that. Sitting in the back of a taxi on the way to Simon's, Nathanial's words kept going around in my head. Maybe this was how it was when things were meant to be. Maybe it wasn't meant to be easy all of the time. Perhaps Madison and I needed the friction and the fire. My head was spinning and that wasn't down to just the alcohol. It was Madison and the fear that by storming out like an angry child having a tantrum I had risked it all. Thank fuck Simon had come to rescue me or I dreaded to think what I could have done. I wouldn't have cheated on her, of that I was certain, but a private strip or show, I couldn't guarantee. Shit! I remembered folding money up and holding it out for one of the strippers. She'd been gorgeous and her body was amazing in her tiny bikini, but compared to my wife, she paled. Even doing it had felt wrong and unnatural. It had also felt like a betrayal of my wife. The woman I loved.

"Change of plan," I suddenly announced. "I need to go home. I need to see Madison, speak to her, listen to her and to tell her that I love her."

I gave the driver the address and although the jolt of the taxi as it abruptly u-turned caused my stomach to lurch, I was determined not to lose the contents of it, nor my wife.

The thirty-minute journey seemed to take forever and as we pulled up to the kerbside on the street where the house my father had shared with Helen was situated, the security gate opened, revealing Madison.

I staggered out and as I prepared to pay the fare and speak to Simon, he got out with me.

"Gideon, she has a bag."

I turned back to the path and saw Madison getting closer and as Simon had said, she was carrying a bag. Not a suitcase, but enough of a bag that said she was leaving.

"No!" I told her.

"You don't tell me what to do." She looked up and down the road, possibly waiting for someone or maybe a taxi.

Mine was already at the bottom of the road.

"Madison, let's talk."

She stood at the kerb and turned to face me. She looked sad and she had been crying. Correction. She was still crying.

"Nothing to talk about, although, you could always call Maria Ferguson if you're at a loose end. She might even send you some snaps of your night out!" She snarled the last three words.

"What?" I was confused. "What had Maria got to do with this?"

A couple of cars drove past, both going too fast. I hated this street. I lived in an apartment, but if I lived in a house, I'd have one off the road, maybe a gated community or better still a private estate. I had no idea why Dad and Helen had chosen such a lovely house on what was essentially a main road.

I was swaying slightly when a van came past and almost pulled me into its path. Madison was passing her phone to Simon who hissed and swore at the screen before showing the images there to me.

"It's not what it looks like." That sounded pathetic even to my own ears. I looked guilty as sin, and I was on several counts, but not what she clearly believed me to be.

"I wonder if that's what your dad told your mum when she discovered his affair with my mother?"

I ignored her attempts to goad me but did respond to defend myself. "I have not slept with her."

She shrugged as if she didn't care, but the sob and shedding of more tears disputed that. "Well, she has an exclusive for Maria Ferguson so I guess time will tell. Not my problem though, Gideon. This was madness from the get-go and the fact that me merely wanting to keep my name results in this . . ." She released a loud huff. "Well, it has proven that for me, a marriage should be a partnership—"

I cut her off. "It is."

She shook her head at me and offered a strange little smile that was something between empathy and laughter aimed directly at me.

"I want a democracy, not a dictatorship."

She prepared to step into the road, heading to a taxi I hadn't realised had arrived.

"Don't go, we need to talk. I swear, nothing happened with the stripper."

She nodded and I thought she might believe me. "I

can't stay, Gideon. If I do, you might just convince me to stay."

Her tears and sobs were freely given now. I stepped forward, reaching for her, but in my drunken state wobbled until I ended up on my knees, still staring across the road as she crossed it.

"Madison," I called to her and she turned, her eyes trained on mine. It was now or never, and I knew I couldn't let her leave without telling her. "I love you."

Her lips curled and I wasn't sure, but I thought this might be my one chance to convince her to stay and to listen to me.

"Stay tonight, to talk."

It could have been the alcohol in my system or the tears I was unashamedly crying but my eyes blurred. However, she was heading back towards me and then, all I heard was the sound of my own screams as the world stopped and my heart broke as I watched the woman I loved being catapulted into the air as a speeding car hit her.

Epilogue

Gideon
Nine months later

I had never known grief like it. Nine long months ago, when Madison had been run over as she attempted to come back to me seemed like a lifetime ago but also still raw. I had sobered up immediately and while Simon called the ambulance, I had rushed to her. I was no medic, but I could see she was in a bad way. The driver had barely registered for me, I simply needed to be with her.

The ambulance crew had been amazing and had arrived in minutes although it had felt much longer. Madison was taken to hospital taped to a stretcher and unconscious. The looks from the medics at the scene and in the hospital had confirmed how bad it was. Her skull was fractured as were several bones in her legs and arms. She had internal bleeding in her abdomen and her brain. They took her into theatre where she had been for almost eight long hours.

Even after she was settled in ICU, the prognosis was poor, and I was told to prepare myself for the worst. She was in a coma that she might never wake from.

I remained at her bedside day after day and eventually the days turned into weeks. I swear I aged thirty years during that time, but I remained with her, talking to her, promising to only ever make her happy if she'd let me.

I was beginning to give up all hope and then, one Saturday morning as I sat watching her, she moved. She'd moved before, but this had been different, it had been more controlled. The staff all thought I was delusional until she did it again, her eyes flickering open this time.

The memory of her looking at me, her voice hoarse as she attempted to speak, still moved me.

"You love me?"

Those had been her first husky words. She cried as she'd said them, but fuck me, I had bawled like a baby as I'd confirmed my feelings for her and then sobbed as she'd spoken again.

"I love you, too."

～

A SLAP ON MY BACK JOLTED ME FROM MY THOUGHTS.

"You okay?" Simon asked, smiling at me.

"Yeah, better than okay."

"Well, you look like a dog with two dicks."

We both laughed.

"I feel like one."

"Who'd have thought that this, today was even possible?"

"Not me," I conceded. With a heavy sigh, emotion rolled over me, very mixed emotions.

"Hey, she is better, all repaired and mad enough to marry you, again."

I couldn't fight the grin spreading across my face. Exactly a year to the day we had first married, we were renewing our vows, but this time, for us, this was the first wedding. This was the one where we meant every word we said. Madison was my other half and without her I had only ever lived a half-life, but no more. I knew I loved her before the accident, but that love had only grown in the aftermath of it from the time when I thought she wouldn't survive, to now, the first day of forever.

John Barrington waved to me from his seat in the congregation. The business side of my father's will was all settled, as of today, but had I lost it all and kept Madison, that would have been worth it. She was worth more than anything else in the world to me.

This was a bigger congregation than last time and no Maria Ferguson. Not because I truly held her responsible for her call to Madison. It was her job I supposed, but more than that, from our original wedding day, I had invited her in, so that was as much on me as her. Nathanial Marks and his wife sat on Madison's side of the congregation and they each waved and smiled. They had been amazing over the last nine months, had become friends to us and Madison was doing business with him now.

My mother appeared and grinned at me. She adored Madison and the fact that my wife made me happy and content just made my mum love her more I think. Mum was the first one to call me out on my shit if she thought I was being unfair to my wife, not that she needed to do that often. My wife was more than capable of standing up for herself. My mum had lost her shit when she found out about me changing Madison's name in the business without her knowledge or consent. She had also been the one to ask which was most important, her carrying my name or her being mine? I had changed everything back the day Madison woke up. I smiled to myself that it was all changing again today, at Madison's request. Now that she felt like she truly was my wife, she wanted to carry my name.

Madison

TODAY WAS MY WEDDING DAY AND I WAS THRILLED. I couldn't wait to be Mrs. Gideon Knight. The irony of how I'd fought it didn't escape me, but I had always said that when I took a man's name it would be because I intended to keep it, and I no longer imagined not being Gideon's wife.

I thought back to that night when I had decided to leave. He had been very drunk, but his words and denials of wrongdoing had seemed entirely genuine. However, I was still going. Needed to. At that point, I wasn't sure how long I was going for, but I needed some time and some space. That plan had and hadn't worked out. I'd had plenty of time away from Gideon by ending up in a coma, but the space hadn't been achieved as he hadn't left my bedside for more than a few minutes for months. I smiled as I recalled one of the nurses telling me that it was a standing joke amongst the staff that the hospital had inadvertently become the headquarters of Knight Inc.

When I regained consciousness Gideon had been the first person I had seen, and nothing had made me happier than the sight of him crying happy tears.

I remembered his last words to me. He loved me. A sentiment he confirmed and that is when I was honest with him and admitted my feelings for him too.

My recovery hadn't been easy, but with each day that passed I had gotten stronger and knowing that Gideon was at my side, physically and emotionally only made my strength and determination grow.

"We haven't got to do this every year have we?" Josie stood next to me wearing a simple but elegant full length silver gown.

I laughed. "No. Last time."

"Good. You know I struggle to wear heels, but it has to be done in a dress like this."

I lifted up my wedding dress and revealed white, lace up trainers. "I beg to differ." I twirled so she could see the satin laces, diamante detail and mine and Gideon's initials intertwined in embroidery into the back of them.

"I think I preferred you two when you just enjoyed the hot sex."

"We still do that too."

She pulled a face of mock horror. "Yeah, that much is clear, isn't it?" She leaned down and positioned her face in front of my belly that had a small swell to it.

I gently ran a hand over it and fell a little more in love with my husband and unborn baby.

"Are you sure about the business and the name change thing?" Josie still wasn't convinced this wasn't something I might regret.

She was wrong though. I was sure, completely. "The name change is easy, the business not so much, but I want to be a good mum and although I could employ someone to run the business, by merging with Marks publishing, my dad's business grows, and I now have the flexibility to work a lot less and spend time with the baby."

"And Gideon was okay with it?"

Gideon still liked to be in control, having a say in every aspect of the business, but where my father's company was concerned, he advised and supported me in whatever decisions I made. "Absolutely. I think he likes the idea of me being at home more and us not having a nanny."

Josie laughed. "Only because you suggested a male nanny who looked like a model from the cover of a magazine."

I couldn't deny it. I had.

"Let's go." I was already striding to the door, ready to get married for what Gideon and I considered the first time.

***

THE SOUND OF MUSIC PLAYED AS I MADE MY WAY DOWN the aisle to where he stood. When I came to a stop next to him, he immediately leaned in and kissed me before stroking a hand across my slightly swollen belly. It was common knowledge that I was pregnant, but had it not been, it would be now.

The celebrant opened the ceremony by welcoming everyone and then paid memorial to my parents and Lucas whom he cited as *seeing something between the bride and groom that they themselves had missed.* Along with Gideon's mother, we both believed that to be the case and that by adding the clause to his will, forcing us to marry, he had intended for us each to discover our missing piece, and we had.

THE END

ABOUT THE AUTHOR

Elle M Thomas was born in the north of England and raised near Birmingham, UK where she still lives with her family. She works in local education and writes in her spare time with dreams of becoming a full-time writer. Whilst still at school, and with a love of writing slightly risqué tales of love and romance, one of her teachers told her that she could be the next Harrold Robins. Elle didn't act on those words for many years. In February 2017, with her first book completed and a dozen others unfinished, she finally took the plunge and self-published the steamy romance, Disaster-in-Waiting.

Elle describes her books as stories filled with chemistry, sensuality, love and sex that she always wanted to read and her characters as three dimensional and flawed.

OTHER TITLES

**<u>Contemporary romance titles
by Elle M Thomas:</u>**

Disaster-in-Waiting
Revealing His Prize

Carrington Siblings Series
(should be read in order)
One Night Or Forever (Mason and Olivia)
Family Affair (Declan and Anita)

Love in Vegas Series
(to be read in order)
Lucky Seven (Book 1)
Pushing His Luck (Book 2)
Lucking Out (Book 3)

Love in Vegas Novellas (to be read in timeline order)

OTHER TITLES

Winters Wishes (takes place during Lucking Out)
Valentine's Vows (takes place around three years after Lucking Out)

Falling Series
(to be read in order)
New Beginnings *(Book 1)*
Still Falling *(Book 2)*
New Beginnings/Falling Series Novellas
(to be read in timeline order)
Old Endings
(prequel to New Beginnings – Eve's Story)

The Nanny Chronicles
(to be read in order)
Single Dad (Gabe and Carrie)
Pinky Promise (Seb and Bea)
Tell Me To Stop (Maurizio and Flora)

Second Chances Duet
Second Chances – Losing the Past
Second Chances – Finding the Future

The Infidelity Trilogy
(to be read in order)
Sex, Lies,
Secrets
And Wives

Erotic romance titles by Elle M Thomas:

The Revelation Series
Days of Discovery – Kate & Marcus Book 1
Events of Endeavour – Kate & Marcus Book 2